SAMI vs. THE NEGATIVE VOICE

written by Sami Kader

with assistance from Laura Schwab

Special contributors:

Melissa Jimenez, MS, LMFT

Kara Walsh, MA, LMFT, PPS

Illustrated by Fanny Liem

This book is dedicated to my children, Christian, Charlotte, Elanor, and William, who inspire me every day, and to my wife, Megan, who has told me, "You got this!" from day one.

Sami was eight.
He was starting grade 2.
The other kids had friends,
And he wanted some, too.

But Sami felt different
From the kids in his grade,
And he became sad
At the jokes that some made.

2

At recess he would watch
As all the kids played,
But Sami wasn't invited,
So alone he stayed.

Sami's teacher decided
One day in the fall
That today they would play
A game of kickball.

When it came to sports,
Kids were pretty mean.
They didn't want to have
Sami on their team.

Young Sami was determined
To show everyone he knew
That he could play sports
And be good at them, too!

The pitcher geared up.
The ball flew off the mound,
But Sami's kick missed,
And he fell on the ground.

7

Laughter burst out.
"That was **AWFUL**!" they said.

The kids pointed and giggled
As Sami turned red.

Sami came home upset
With his heart bruised and torn,
And that was the day
The Negative Voice was born.

The kids had all laughed.
They had been so unkind,
But worse than that now
Were the thoughts in his mind.

"I'm awful! I'm terrible!"
"I should never have tried!"
"I can't do anything!"
He said as he cried.

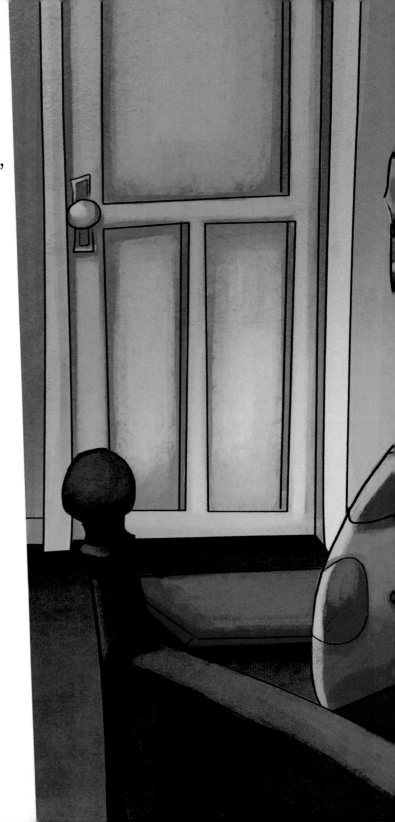

From that day on,
It stuck like glue.
Wherever Sami went,
The Negative Voice went, too.

It followed him through grades
Three, four, and five.
Sami couldn't lose that Voice,
No matter how hard he tried.

It was there during tests.
"You can't do this!" it said.
It was so hard to think with
The Negative Voice in his head.

Apple

Butte

It was there during recess
As all the kids played,
Saying, "You'll never have friends
Like those other kids made!"

So Sami went home
And just sat on his couch.
The Negative Voice made him lonely
And kind of a grouch.

His sister couldn't help.
She didn't know what to do,
So she told her friend Ronny,
Hoping maybe he knew.

When Ronny showed up,
Young Sami complained.
He just wanted to hide
And not deal with the pain.

Ronny thought to himself,
"I have no other choice.
I must help Sami stop
That Negative Voice!"

Ronny told Sami,
"It doesn't matter
what they say.
It's what you think of you,
So make that Voice go away!"

So Sami tried thinking
About positive words,
But since he didn't believe them,
The Negative Voice he still heard.

Ronny scratched his head.
He'd have to try harder.
That Negative Voice was tough,
But Ronny was smarter.

"Let's try something else.
Now repeat after me,
I got this! " he shouted,
"Just say it! You'll see!"

"I got this?" Sami said
As he tried to repeat it.
"No! Not like that!" Ronny said,
"You have to **BELIEVE** it!"

23

So Sami took a deep breath
And closed both his eyes.
"I GOT THIS!"
he yelled,
Much to Ronny's surprise.

"That's it!" Ronny cheered.
"You got this!" he repeated,
But he knew Sami's battle
Was not yet completed.

Sami went back to school
The very next day,
And he tried not to think
The negative way.

"I can do this! I got this,"
He made himself say,
"I'll never give up!"
"I am awesome today!"

And as he continued,
The Negative Voice got smaller.
When Sami entered his class,
He was walking a little taller.

The kids all noticed
Something seemed out of place.
Sami looked happy –
He had a smile on his face!

Sami's thoughts turned positive,
And his confidence grew.
He began to like himself,
And the other kids did, too.

When Sami would hear
The Voice say, "Don't try it!"
He'd say his positive words,
And The Negative Voice
would be quiet.

No longer was Sami
Sad and blue every day.
When he thought positive things,
The Negative Voice went away!

Sami took what he learned
From the battle he went through,
And he hopes that these words
Can help someone like you.

So don't let The Negative Voice
Come from you or another.
Speak positive words
To yourself, friends, and others.

And when you meet people
With nothing positive to say,
Tell them, "You got this!"
And brighten their day.

About the Negative Voice

The Negative Voice is not an actual monster. The Negative Voice represents the words we say or think to ourselves that prevent us from being able to try new things or feel confident in ourselves. Some examples of the Negative Voice are: "I can't do it," "I'm not good enough," or "I should just give up."

Sami's Tips

- When we hear the Negative Voice from other people, the worst thing we can do is start to believe it. If you hear negativity, just remind yourself that those words aren't true. Practice telling yourself positive things every day, like "**I can do this**," "**I've got this**," and "**I'll never give up**."

- Sometimes the Negative Voice becomes so big in our minds, that we wind up passing it along by saying negative things to other people. Not only do we need to make sure we tell ourselves positive words - we also need to use positive words when speaking to others.

Questions & Conversation Starters

- What were some things the Negative Voice said to Sami?

- How did the Negative Voice make Sami feel?

- Do you have a Negative Voice sometimes? If so, what does it say? What does it sound like?

- How does your Negative Voice make you feel?

- How did Ronny help Sami?

- What did Sami do to overcome the Negative Voice?

- What are some things you can say to help the Negative Voice go away?

- Who in your life can help you in the way that Ronny helped Sami?

NEVER FORGET - YOU GOT THIS!

About Sami Kader

Sami Kader is a motivational speaker, children's book author, and founder of Sami's Circuit, an elementary school program that brings social-emotional learning to life.

Leveraging the lessons he learned while battling childhood obesity, troubles at home, and years of traumatic bullying by his peers, Sami creates a unique, personal connection with students and families, empowering them to overcome any obstacle they face by using the powers they already have.

Since 2010, Sami's humorous yet genuine approach has compelled children and adults to laugh while they learn. His high-energy delivery and enthusiasm ignite his audience, getting them up and moving, and leaving them with tools and mindsets they can implement into their daily lives.

Sami has received local and national media coverage for his work with hundreds of thousands of students all over California. His video-based school program, "Sami's Circuit On Demand," has allowed his mission to expand nationwide, working seamlessly with both in-class and distance learning models.

For more information about Sami or Sami's Circuit, visit **www.samiscircuit.com.**

Made in the USA
Las Vegas, NV
23 March 2023

69518676R00026